Sushi
for Kids

A children's introduction
to Japan's favorite food

by Kaoru Ono

translated by
Peter Howlett & Richard McNamara

TUTTLE PUBLISHING
Boston • Rutland, Vermont • Tokyo

Today is Atsushi's grandfather's 72nd birthday and the entire family has gathered to celebrate. The dining table is covered with lots of wonderful dishes, including two large trays of sushi. Atsushi has never seen so many kinds of sushi.

"Dad, what's that pinkish one?" asks Atsushi.

"It's tuna," answers Father.

"And that red one, what kind of fish is that?" asks Atsushi again.

"That's tuna too," says Father.

"And the white one?"

"That's sea bream."

Atsushi has so many questions, his father doesn't even have time to get one bite of the delicious sushi.

3

The following Sunday, Atsushi's father decides to take him on a grand sushi tour. So off they go to the local sushi shop. The owner is Mr Kaneko, an old classmate of Atsushi's father. Atsushi bows to Mr Kaneko and says hello.

Mr Kaneko says, "Atsushi, your father tells me you have all sorts of questions about sushi."
"That's right, Mr Kaneko," says Atsushi, "I love sushi and I want to know more about it."

Atsushi climbs up onto the highstool. There in front of him is a long glass case filled with all sorts of sushi toppings.

Pointing to a red topping, Atsushi asks, "That's tuna, right?"
"Good, Atsushi, you know your fish, don't you!" says Mr Kaneko. "But do you know what a tuna looks like?"
"Umm . . ." ponders Atsushi.
"Do you think it's a big or small fish?" asks Mr Kaneko again.
"Umm . . . I give up," says Atsushi.
Mr Kaneko laughs and says, "You've never seen the real thing, have you? You've only seen tuna that has been sliced up. Well, first things first. Let's go to the fish market tomorrow. What do you say?"
"Great idea, Mr Kaneko, I'd love to go!" replies Atsushi.

I have to close
my eyes. It all
looks so good!

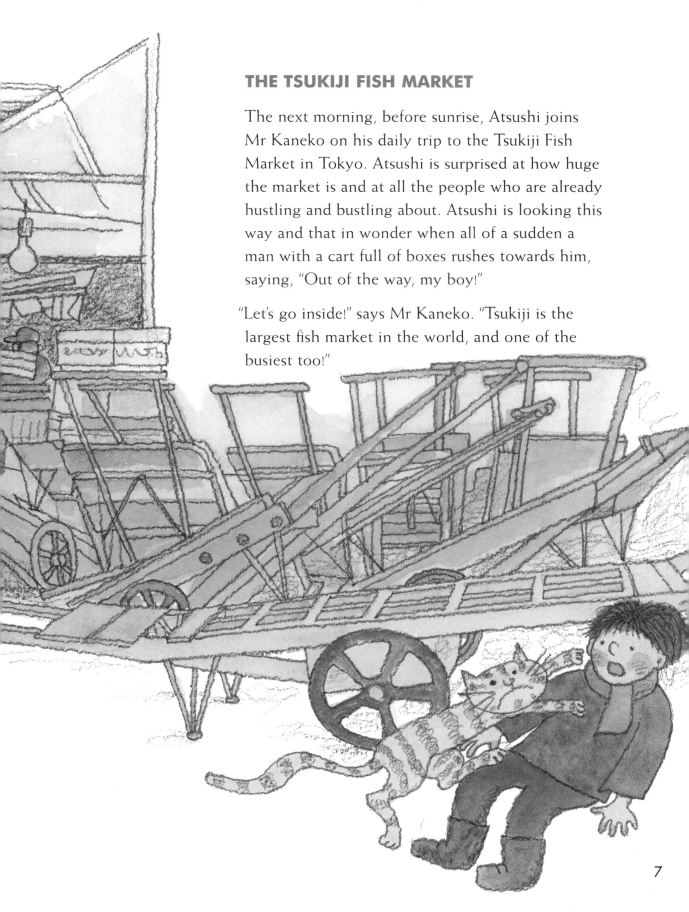

THE TSUKIJI FISH MARKET

The next morning, before sunrise, Atsushi joins Mr Kaneko on his daily trip to the Tsukiji Fish Market in Tokyo. Atsushi is surprised at how huge the market is and at all the people who are already hustling and bustling about. Atsushi is looking this way and that in wonder when all of a sudden a man with a cart full of boxes rushes towards him, saying, "Out of the way, my boy!"

"Let's go inside!" says Mr Kaneko. "Tsukiji is the largest fish market in the world, and one of the busiest too!"

Inside the market, Atsushi sees many tuna lined up on the floor. The fresh tuna have been caught in waters near Japan. The frozen tuna come from over 60 different countries, including America, Africa and Peru. The ratio of fresh fish to frozen fish is about 20% to 80%.

The place of origin and the weight of the fish are written on these tags.

This one says Cape Town. That means this fish came all the way from Africa!

THE WHOLESALE MERCHANT

At 4 a.m. the wholesale merchant takes fresh and frozen tuna from the fishing boats and lines them up. Next, he cuts off the tails so the flesh can be examined.

THE DISTRIBUTOR

The distributor goes around and carefully checks each tuna's place of origin, weight and quality. He then decides which fish he wants to buy.

BIDDING

At 5 a.m. a bell is rung and the bidding begins. The distributor buys the tuna from the wholesale merchant. If there are more than two bidders, the one who bids the highest price wins the deal and gets the fish.

THE RETAILER

The distributor takes the tuna he has just bought to his shop in the market, where he cuts it into smaller portions. He then sells these to retailers such as the owners of fish shops, sushi shops and restaurants.

9

In another part of the market, Atsushi watches as a distributor cuts up the tuna he has purchased. He cuts frozen fish with an electric saw and fresh fish with a carving knife and a long, slender knife that looks like a sword. At times he also uses a hatchet and a saw.

One tuna weighs about 550 lbs (250 kg). That's about 12 times the weight of Atsushi. A slice of fish used in *nigirizushi* (hand-molded sushi) weighs about ½ oz (14 g), so can you imagine how many servings of *nigirizushi* you can make from one tuna? Even if you subtract the weight of the head, tail, fins and bones, that comes to over 10,000 servings.

11

Ouch!

Mr Kaneko says to Atsushi, "The fish from the Tsukiji Fish Market is sent to shops throughout Japan and the rest of the world!"

Mr Kaneko also buys some squid, sea bream, octopus, mackerel, shrimp and shellfish, and many more types of fish. Atsushi helps him to carry all of this back to the sushi shop.

14

When they arrive at the shop, Mr Kaneko cooks some rice and lines up all the fish he has bought in the glass case.

Using a sharp knife, Mr Kaneko slices the tuna into several smaller pieces, then slices these into bite-sized pieces. Next, he spreads out the cooked rice in a shallow wooden bowl and pours a vinegar-sugar dressing over it. Fanning the rice to cool it, he mixes the dressing evenly through the rice by using a wooden spatula. Then, taking a small handful of the rice, Mr Kaneko shapes it into a ball. Taking a slice of fish he dabs some *wasabi* (Japanese horseradish) on it and then places it on the rice. He presses it all together and places two servings in front of Atsushi, saying, "Here you go! One *chutoro*."

Atsushi exclaims, "I never would have imagined that this sushi came from that big fish!" He dips his sushi in a dish of soy sauce and pops it into his mouth. "Umm, yummy! But Mr Kaneko, why did you call this piece of tuna *chutoro*?"

"That's because each part of a tuna has a different name and taste," says Mr Kaneko.

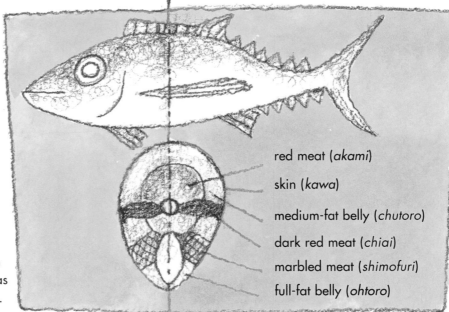

red meat (*akami*)

skin (*kawa*)

medium-fat belly (*chutoro*)

dark red meat (*chiai*)

marbled meat (*shimofuri*)

full-fat belly (*ohtoro*)

The flesh of each part of a tuna has a different name.

FISH USED IN SUSHI

Tuna live far out from shore in the open seas. They are very big fish and there are many different types of tuna.

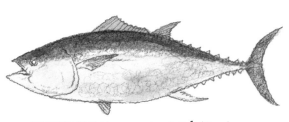

BIGEYE TUNA grow to 6.5 ft (2 m) and weigh up to 450 lbs (200 kg).

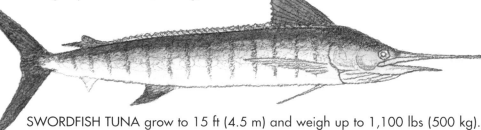

SWORDFISH TUNA grow to 15 ft (4.5 m) and weigh up to 1,100 lbs (500 kg).

Sea bream is expensive and often and eaten at festive times.

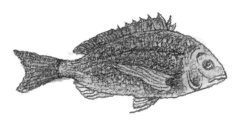

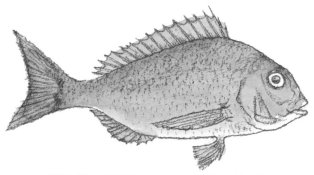

BLACK PORGY grow to 20 in (50 cm).

RED SEA BREAM grow to 40 in (1 m).

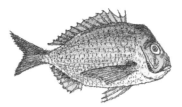

KIDAI grow to 16 in (40 cm).

PARROT FISH have black stripes and grow to 26 in (65 cm).

Flatfish and flounders live on the sandy ocean floors and their coloring resembles the sand. They lie flat on the sea bottom and swim by fluttering across the ocean floor. They are very similar but can be distinguished by a number of ways; flatfish face right whereas flounders face left. Flatfish also have small mouths whereas flounders have large mouths.

BLUEFIN TUNA grow to 10 ft (3 m) and weigh up to 770 lbs (350 kg).

FLATFISH 16 in (40 cm)

FLOUNDER 31 in (80 cm)

Squid and octopus live in oceans throughout the world. Squid have ten legs and octopus have eight legs.

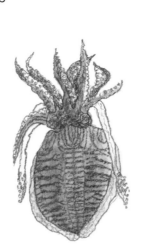

HOTARUIKA
3 in (7 cm)

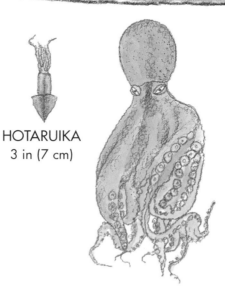

SAGITTATE
12 in (30 cm)

YARIIKA
12 in (30 cm)

MONGOHIKA
8 in (20 cm)

COMMON OCTOPUS
31 in (80 cm)

MACKEREL

SHRIMP

SARDINE

MANTIS SHRIMP

EG

SEA URCHIN

CLAM

PEN SHELL

ABALONE

ARK SHELL

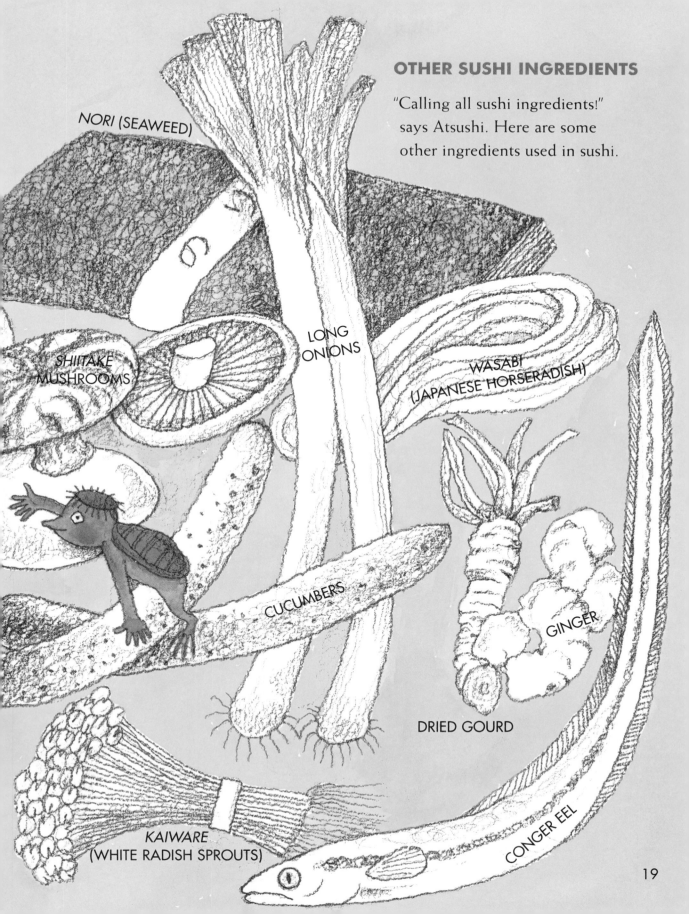

OTHER SUSHI INGREDIENTS

"Calling all sushi ingredients!" says Atsushi. Here are some other ingredients used in sushi.

NORI (SEAWEED)

LONG ONIONS

SHIITAKE MUSHROOMS

WASABI (JAPANESE HORSERADISH)

CUCUMBERS

GINGER

DRIED GOURD

KAIWARE (WHITE RADISH SPROUTS)

CONGER EEL

19

THE ORIGINS OF SUSHI

"Sushi has a long history, Atsushi," says Mr Kaneko.

It originated over 2,000 years ago in the mountainous regions of Southeast Asia. It was originally a method used to preserve fish. It is said that sushi first came to Japan with the introduction of wet rice culture.

Indochina

The Philippines

The Malay Peninsula

Kalimantan

Sumatra

Sulawesi

Java

This original sushi was called *narezushi* and was made by packing salted fish in cooked rice, which was then left to ferment for about a year. The fermented rice became sour and this was what helped to preserve the fish. In this method the rice is discarded and only the pickled fish is eaten. In Shiga Prefecture they still make a variant of this sushi called *funazushi*.

Some people thought it was wasteful to throw away this rice, so they made a variation of this process by shortening the waiting time to seven days and eating both the fish and the rice. This type of sushi is called *namanare*.

The waiting time was further shortened to three days, then one day, and then one night. Finally, the pickling process was dropped altogether and instead the method of serving raw fish on vinegared rice was introduced. This sushi can be eaten right away and is called *nigirizushi*.

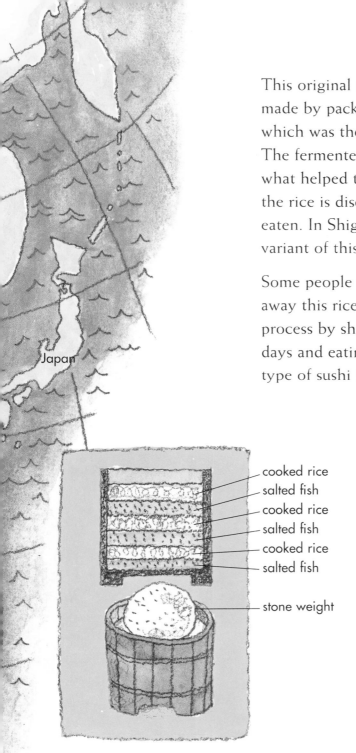

Japan

cooked rice
salted fish
cooked rice
salted fish
cooked rice
salted fish

stone weight

narezushi

ALL ABOUT SUSHI SHOPS

About 350 years ago, *namanare* sushi and *nigirizushi* were sold by peddlers called *sushuri*.

Sushi stall

Sushi peddler

Sushi peddlers packed sushi in tubs which they carried on their shoulders or held in their hands. They went from door to door to sell their sushi. They used such fish as carp, mackerel, gizzard shad, salmon, yellowtail, trout, sea bream and shrimp.

About 200 years ago *inarizushi* stalls first appeared. *Inarizushi* consists of a pocket of deep-fried bean curd (*aburaage*) filled with vinegared rice.

22

Fish seller

Inarizushi stall

Letter carrier

Sushi peddler

Sushi peddler

For busy people living in towns, sushi was a simple and fast meal. For this reason its popularity grew. Sushi was first sold by peddlers and at sushi stalls, but fancy sushi shops soon appeared which offered their cuisine at very high prices.

Then about 150 years ago the Shogunate Government of Edo handed down an official notice stating that all extravagant styles of living were to be banned. It is said that at this time over 200 fancy sushi shop owners ignored this notice and were punished.

All extravagance is banned!

I order you to pay a fine of 5 kan and sentence you to 60 days in hand chains.

Tohyama Kagemoto, the Honorable Judge of Kitamachi

Lord Mizuno Tadakuni

LET'S MAKE SUSHI
*Adult help is necessary for these preliminary steps.

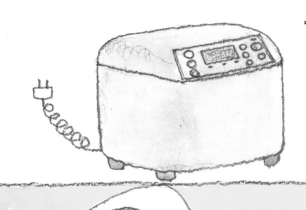

*1. Boiling the Rice
- 3 cups of rice (for 5 servings)
  Boil the rice so that it is a bit
  on the hard side.

3. Preparing the Rice
Cool and spread out the cooked rice in
a wooden bowl. Pour the dressing
(2) evenly over the rice. Using
a spatula, mix in the dressing
using swift motions. Now
here's a job for you kids. Fan
the rice as the dressing is
being mixed in so as to cool it.

LET'S MAKE NIGIRIZUSHI

1. Take a small handful of sushi rice and shape it into a firm ball.
2. Dab a small amount of *wasabi* on the slice of *tane* fish.
3. Put the rice on top of the tane and press down. Next, turn it over
   so the fish is on top and press the sides and top. The rice should
   form a firm oblong shape. Now it's ready to eat.

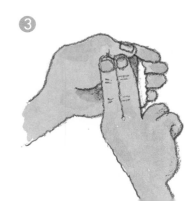

*2. Making the Sushi Vinegar Dressing

- 3 tablespoons of vinegar
- 2 tablespoons of sugar
- 1 tablespoon of salt
  Put these ingredients in a pan and heat
  until the sugar dissolves, then cool.

*4. Slicing the Toppings

Slice up the fish, egg and other ingredients to be used as toppings for *nigirizushi*. The toppings are called *tane*.

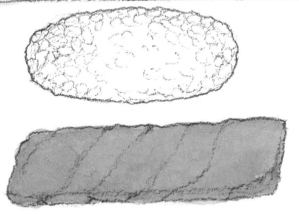

Okay kids, your turn next. Take a handful of rice about the size of the picture and press into shape. Sprinkle some vinegar on your hands before you do this so that the rice won't stick to your hands. Put the *tane* on the rice and press together. If you like things a little "hot" dab some *wasabi* on the *tane* before you put it on the rice.

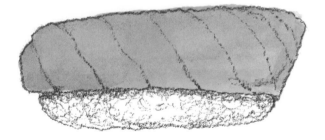

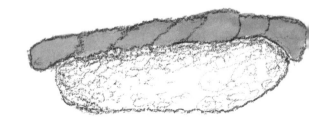

LET'S MAKE NORIMAKI

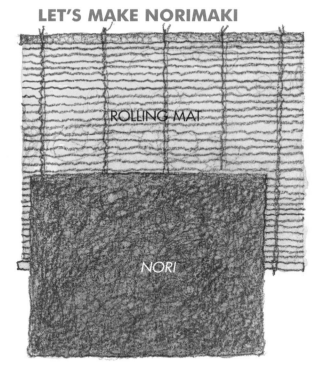

ROLLING MAT

NORI

SUSHI RICE

EGG

GOURD

SPINACH

CUCUMBER

Norimaki is sushi wrapped in a seaweed roll.

You will need:
- 1 rolling mat
- 1 sheet of *nori*
- 1 small bowl of sushi rice for a small *norimaki*
- 1 large bowl of sushi rice for a fat *norimaki*

1. Place the rolling mat on the table and lay one sheet of *nori* on the mat.
2. Spread an even layer of sushi rice across the *nori*.
3. Lay the fillings on top of the rice. Use egg, gourd, spinach or cucumber, or whatever filling you like.
4. Lift up the bottom edge of the rolling mat and roll everything together.
5. After rolling to the other edge, grip the rolling mat and press firmly to mold.
6. Remove the rolling mat and slice into bite-sized pieces to finish.

   To make a thick roll, use more sushi rice and *tane*.

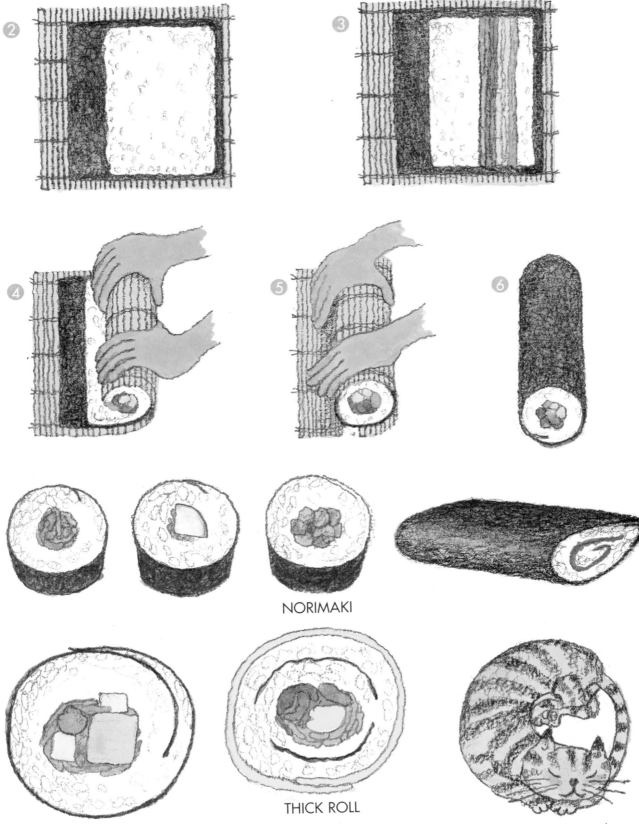

NORIMAKI

THICK ROLL

Don't roll me too!

LET'S MAKE GUNKANMAKI (BATTLESHIP ROLL)

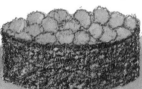
ikura (salmon roe)

kobashira (shell pillars)

1. Cut a sheet of *nori* into thin strips.

2. Wrap a strip of *nori* around a handful of sushi rice to make a shape that resembles a battleship.

LET'S MAKE INARIZUSHI

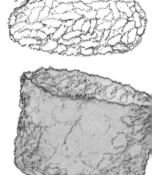

Inarizushi are sushi made with *aburaage* (deep-fried beancurd sheets). You can buy *aburaage* from an Asian supermarket or grocery shop.

*1. Boil the *aburaage* in a *dashi* (fish) broth with soy sauce and vinegar.

*2. Cut a piece of *aburaage* in half and open it so that it forms a pocket.

 3. Stuff the pocket with some sushi rice and roll over the top to seal it.

LET'S MAKE TEMAKIZUSHI

Temakizushi are hand-rolled sushi.

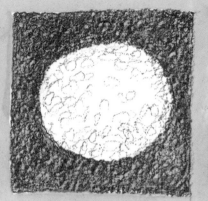

1. Cut a sheet of *nori* into quarters.

2. Place some sushi rice in the center of the *nori* and flatten the rice.

3. Lay the *tane* across the rice. You can use cucumber or tuna.

(sea urchin roe) *hotaruika* (firefly squid)

3. Place your *tane* on the sushi rice.

Wow, it's sushi time!
I want this one!

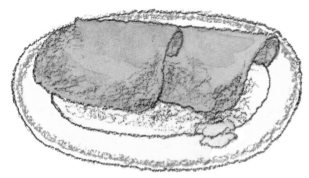

Let's eat sushi!

4. Roll everything together
to make a *temakizushi*.

Time to eat!

The following week Atsushi takes two of his friends to the fish market, but this time he is the guide. Today sushi is loved the world over, not only for its excellent taste but also because it is very healthy. Enjoy sushi but please remember that it first came about long ago as a way of preserving a precious food source. So let's always be thankful and savor each bite of sushi!

Author and Illustrator

Kaoru Ono was born in Tokyo and is a graduate of the Tokyo National University of Fine Arts and Music. She has written and drawn many children's books, including *Spring Breezes Huff and Puff, The Broken Egg, The Mouse's Bride, Playing With Shadows, The Story of the Bridge, Trop and the Jumping Contest* and *Non-non-nonta and the Little Rabbit*. She has also illustrated *The Bear's Tail, The Cat and the Rooster, The Silver Bracelet, The Rhinoceros Called Rhinoo* and *The Bee and the Dream*. Ms Ono is a member of the Tokyo-based artists' group Shinseisaku Kyoukai and is active in designing public monuments. She is also an honorary professor of the Tokyo University of Art and Design. Ms Ono resides in Tokyo.

Translators

Peter Howlett was born and raised in Hokkaido. He is an EFL teacher at Hakodate La Salle Junior & Senior High Schools. He is also the chairperson of the Southern Hokkaido Natural Energy Initiative, a group that promotes the use of alternative energy. **Richard McNamara** is the director of the Aso Wildcats environmental group (AsoWildcats@hotmail.com) and specializes in the poetry of Edmund Spenser and the psychology of stress and clinical biofeedback.

Peter and Richard are officials of the Dr Wildcat Committee, a group dedicated to publicizing environmental issues through the works of Miyazawa Kenji, Vandana Shiva, David Suzuki and Oiwa Kenbo, among others. They are also regular contributors to the *Shukan Kinyobi* magazine and have also translated the popular *Guri and Gura* and *Little Daruma* children's books for Tuttle Publishing.

Published by Tuttle Publishing,
an imprint of Periplus Editions (HK) Ltd.

Text & Illustrations © Kaoru Ono, 1997
First published in 1998 by Fukuinkan Shoten
Publishers, Inc., Tokyo, Japan
First Tuttle edition, 2003

LCC Card No. 2002108056
ISBN 0-8048-3346-X
Printed in Singapore

Distributed by:

Japan
Tuttle Publishing
Yaekari Building, 3F
5-4-12 Osaki, Shinagawa-ku
Tokyo 141-0032
Tel: (03) 5437 0171, Fax: (03) 5437 0755
E-mail: tuttle-sales@gol.com

North America
Tuttle Publishing
Airport Industrial Park
364 Innovation Drive
North Clarendon, VT 05759-9436
Tel: (802) 773 8930, Fax: (802) 773 6993
E-mail: info@tuttlepublishing.com

Asia Pacific
Berkeley Books Pte. Ltd.
130 Joo Seng Road #06-01/03
Singapore 368357
Tel: (65) 6280 1330, Fax: (65) 6280 6290
E-mail: inquiries@periplus.com.sg

おじいちゃんのお誕生日にだいすきなおすしを食べたあっちゃん。お父さんとおすし屋さんや魚市場をめぐりながら、おすしのことを勉強します。お魚のひみつやおすしの歴史を解き明かしたら、みんなでおいなりさんやのりまきをつくってみよう！

文・絵：小野かおる

東京生まれ。東京芸術大学油絵科卒業。絵本の代表作は「はるかぜとぷう」、「われたたまご」、「オンロックがやってくる」、「おかぐら」、「はしをわたらずはしわたれ」（いずれも福音館書店）など多数。スペースデザイナーとしても活躍し、モニュメントの制作などにも意欲的に取り組んでいる。東京芸術大学名誉教授。新制作協会会員。

訳：ピーター・ハウレット
北海道生まれ。函館ラ・サール中・高等学校で教鞭を執る。

リチャード・マクナマラ　イギリス生まれ。阿蘇ワイルド・キャッツの代表として活動するかたわら、阿蘇ワイルド・キャッツラジオ局を運営。阿蘇在住、大学講師。

二人は環境団体「山猫博士の会」のメンバー。宮沢賢治やヴァンダナ・シヴァ等の作品を通じて、環境問題に取り組んでいる。絵本「ぐりとぐら」、「だるまちゃん」シリーズ（タトル出版刊）の翻訳も担当。